ROPOS

Dedication

In celebration of Mark Stoermer,
who generously shared his gift for
turning science into art.

www.mascotbooks.com

ROPOS and the Underwater Volcano

Photographs in this book are provided courtesy of the University of Washington, Ocean Observatories Initiative, the U.S. National Science Foundation, and the Canadian Scientific Submersible Facility. They were taken during VISIONS'11-15 expeditions, led by Chief Scientists J.R. Delaney and D.S. Kelley.

robotsdiscover.com

For more information, please contact:
Mascot Books
620 Herndon Parkway, Suite 320
Herndon, VA 20170
info@mascotbooks.com

Library of Congress Control Number: 2018900624

CPSIA Code: PRT0818A
ISBN-13: 978-1-68401-406-4

Printed in the United States

ROPOS AND THE
UNDERWATER
VOLCANO

Dana Manalang

Illustrated by Hunter Hadaway

My name is ROPOS. I help scientists explore.

I can dive deep to the seafloor.

In the water, there's so much to see,

like fish, plants, and rocks.

Come along with me!

I start from the boat and hope for nice weather.
They lower me down on my very long tether.
I use my thrusters to turn left and right.
It gets dark deep down, so I turn on my lights.

With my cameras, I take pictures of things all around
so the people above can see what I've found.
Down through my tether instructions are sent:
"dive down," "turn around," or "start your ascent."

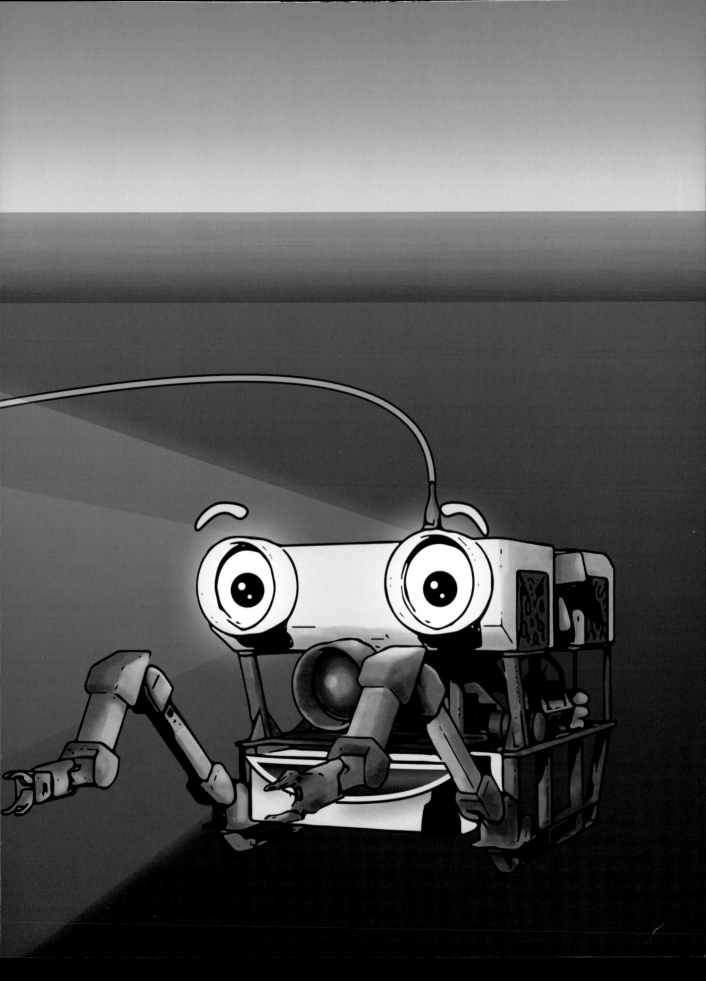

Now here is a fact not all may know:
Deep under the water there are volcanoes.
That's why we're here—to discover the fate
of a volcano that sits between tectonic plates.

Scientists think there has been an eruption.

Their sensors have measured a great disruption.

I'll swim all the way down—it's a long way to go!

We'll learn as much as we can about this volcano.

In other places the seafloor is soft like a bed,
but here it's covered with black rocks instead.
The rocks started out as hot lava flows,
and when they touched the cold water, they froze.

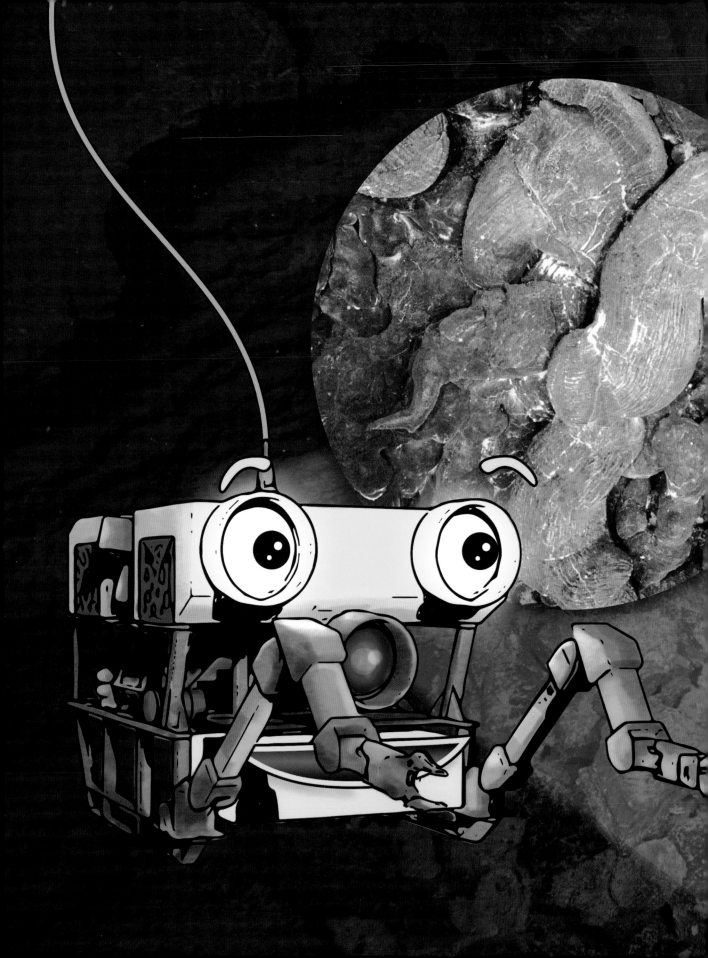

If you look right here, the rocks have sharp edges,
but just over there, they've collapsed and formed ledges.
There are pillowy rocks that are shaped nice and round,
and shiny new flows like glass on the ground.

Wait just a minute! I see little white flakes.

A sure sign that the seafloor has had a good shake.

So I'll turn down my thrusters to swim much slower.

Let's take a look at this amazing snow blower.

It's not really snow! The white stuff is alive,
and it makes a nice meal on which creatures can thrive.
Like these five-legged critters who never go far.
They're spiny and round—brittle sea stars.

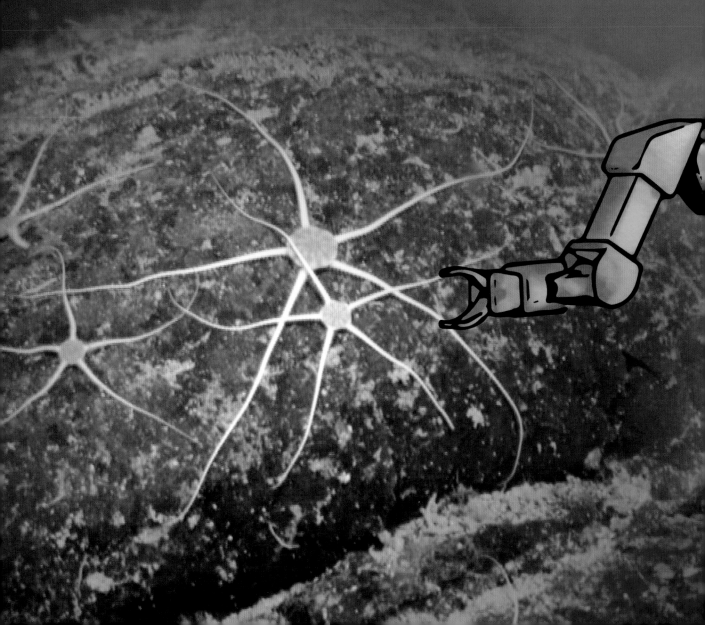

Or this dumbo octopus! Let's try to get near.

It has fins on its head that look like big ears!

And of course, there's the one who uses pinchers to grab.

With long legs and a shell, it's a spider crab.

Over here is a structure that's easy to spot.
I can tell from my sensors that the fluid here's hot.
It flows up from the seafloor with a sulfury scent
and forms a great towering hydrothermal vent!

Some interesting creatures call this vent home, like these tube worms and palm worms you'll never see roam.

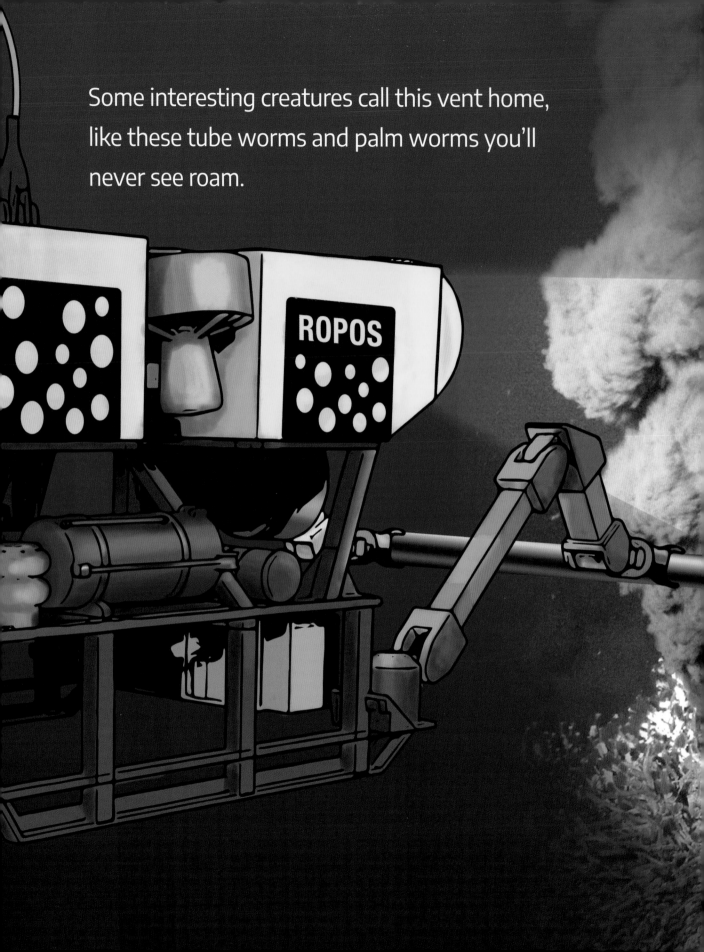

It's amazing they don't seem to mind the high heat.
They just stretch out their plumes when it's time to eat.

Now we've learned quite a lot; a long journey it's been.

It's time to swim up, so my thrusters I'll spin.

But before I can leave, I'd better recover

a sample to help the scientists discover

...what makes this volcano erupt or stay silent
and what will awaken this large sleeping giant.

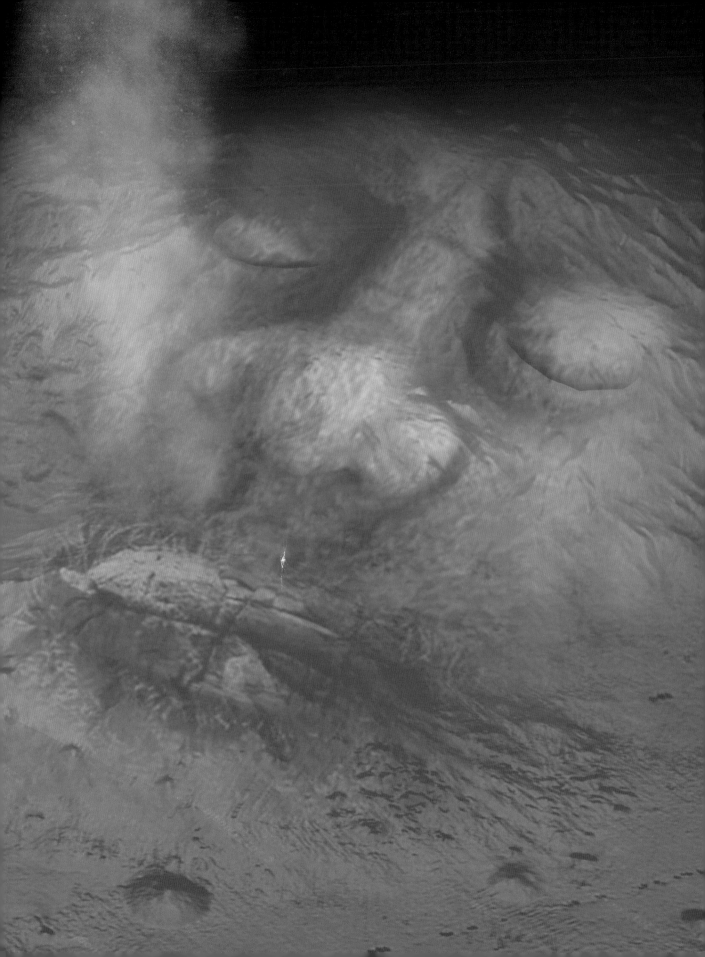

Glossary

Hydrothermal vent: A place where hot, mineral-rich fluid flows up through the Earth's crust

ROPOS: Remotely Operated Platform for Ocean Sciences (ROPOS is a type of ROV)

ROV: Remotely Operated Vehicle

Tectonic plate: A gigantic piece of rock that makes up part of the Earth's surface

Tether: The long cable that connects an ROV to a ship

Thruster: A propeller that spins and moves the ROV through the water

About ROPOS

ROPOS is one of the world's most capable scientific underwater robotic systems. Operated by the Canadian Scientific Submersible Facility, ROPOS travels with a team of engineers all over the world and has helped thousands of researchers explore and discover more about our world's oceans. For more information about ROPOS, check out **www.ropos.com**.

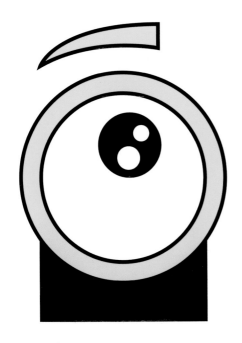
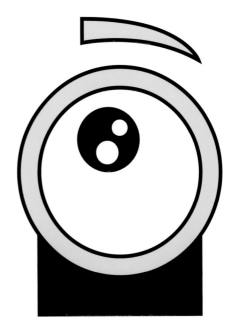

Dana Manalang has been working with underwater systems as an engineer in the Seattle area for over a decade, though her love of the sea goes back as far as she can remember. A mother of two, Dana enjoys sharing her enthusiasm for all things aquatic and robotic with her kids and anyone else who will listen. Her favorite part about working at sea is the thrill of the unknown. At any moment, exotic creatures or events can turn ordinary work days into extraordinary explorations. She hopes that *ROPOS and the Underwater Volcano* conveys that sense of adventure to readers both young and old.

Hunter Hadaway combines his prodigious artistic and computer visualization skills to transform scientific data into graphical representations that are both scientifically useful and visually appealing. His work has been featured in numerous technical publications and educational websites. Additional artistic help and editing was provided by Hyde Hadaway, Hunter's 11 year old son. In his down time, Hunter enjoys spending time with his family and taking advantage of all that the Pacific Northwest has to offer.